Ladybird Reader

The Wizard of Oz
Activity Book

Written by Catrin Morris

Song lyrics on page 16 written by Pippa Mayfield

Illustrated by Richard Johnson

- 🎵 Singing *
- 📖 Reading
- 💬 Speaking
- ❓ Critical thinking
- abc Spelling
- ✏️ Writing
- 🎧 Listening *

* To complete these activities, listen to tracks 2, 3, and 4 of the audio download available at **www.ladybird.com/ladybirdreaders**

1. Look at the pictures. Circle the people and animals you see.

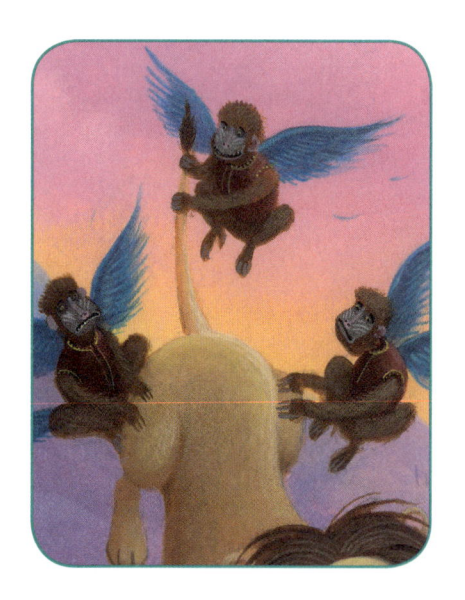

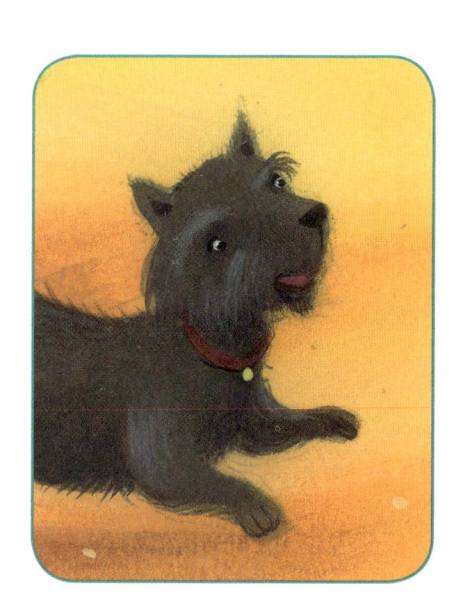

(Dorothy)	girl	tiger
birds	king	tin man
Horrible Witch	lion	tin woman
cat	flying monkeys	uncle
dad	mom	Toto
dog	scarecrow	Wizard of Oz

2 Choose the correct words and write them on the lines.

Toto   wizard   lion

Dorothy   scarecrow   tin man

1 Many years ago, there was a little girl called ……Dorothy…… .

2 She lived with her aunt, her uncle, and her little dog, ……………… .

3 "Hello, I'm a ……………… . My head is full of straw."

4 "Hello, I'm the ……………… . I want to ask the wizard for a heart."

5 Suddenly, an angry ……………… jumped in front of them.

6 "We're going to the Emerald City to see the ……………… ."

3 Work with a friend. Look at the picture and talk about it.

Example:

Where is Dorothy looking?

Dorothy is looking under the house.

4 Listen and put a ✓ by the correct sentence.

1 a "You must go to see the Wizard of Oz." ✓

   b "You must travel along the yellow brick road."

2 a "Can you come with me?"

   b "Can I come with you?"

3 a "Where are you all going?"

   b "Where are you going?"

4 a "I'd like a brain."

   b "I'd like a heart."

5 a "I want to go home."

   b "I just want to go home."

6 a "Please will you help?"

   b "Please will you help us?"

7 a "Now I can think."

   b "Now I can love."

* To complete this activity, listen to track 2 of the audio download available at www.ladybird.com/ladybirdreaders

5 Look at the pictures. Look at the letters. Put a ✓ in the correct box.

1 
- a heat ☐
- b heart ✓

2 
- a which ☐
- b witch ☐

3 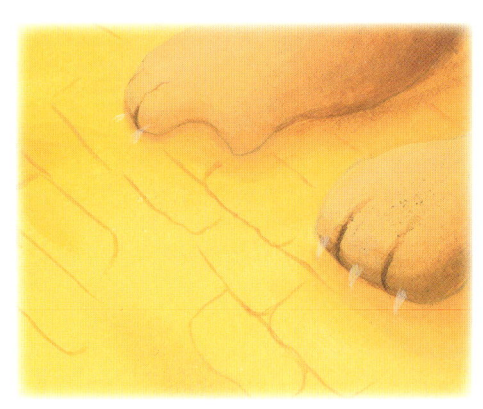
- a brick road ☐
- b break road ☐

4 
- a time ☐
- b tin ☐

5 
- a stone ☐
- b storm ☐

6 
- a bucket ☐
- b pocket ☐

6 Look and read. Circle the correct picture.

1 Where does Dorothy want to be?

a (circled) b c

2 Who are Dorothy's friends?

a b c

3 Who isn't brave?

a b c

4 Which has got the strongest magic?

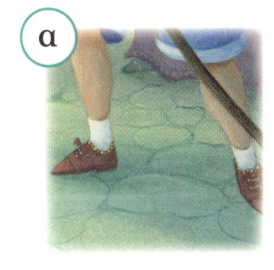

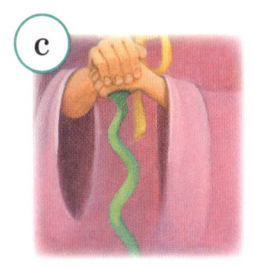

a b c

5 Who helps Dorothy get home?

a b c

7 Work with a friend. Ask and answer questions about the pictures.

Example:

Whose beard is this?

It's the Wizard of Oz's beard.

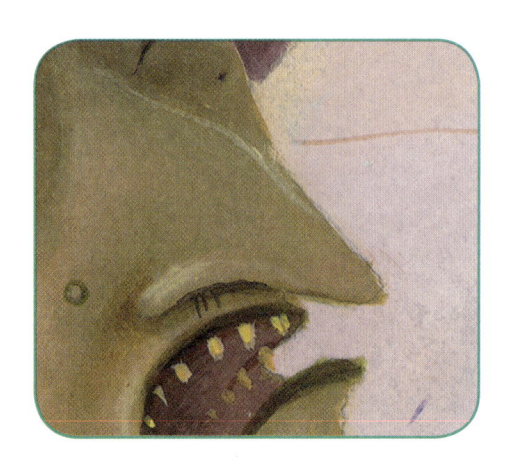

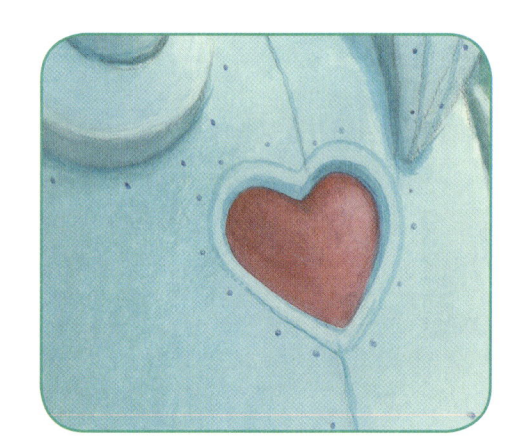

8 Look and read. Circle the correct word.

1 "I just (**want**)/ **don't want** to go home to Kansas," said Dorothy.

2 "I **will** / **won't** help you," said the wizard.

3 "But first, you **must** / **mustn't** help me. Go and kill the last Horrible Witch in Oz."

4 Dorothy and her friends **were** / **weren't** very happy.

5 Could they kill the last Horrible Witch? It **would** / **wouldn't** be easy.

9 Look at the picture and read the questions. Write complete sentences. 📖 ✏️

> Dorothy, Toto, the scarecrow, the tin man, and the lion went to find the Horrible Witch's castle.
>
> Suddenly, the witch's flying monkeys came! They carried Dorothy, her friends, and Toto to the witch's castle.

1 Who came suddenly?

The witch's flying monkeys came suddenly.

2 How many flying monkeys were holding the lion?

....

3 Which part of Toto's body was a flying monkey holding?

....

4 Was the lion feeling brave?

....

5 Was Dorothy feeling happy?

....

10

10 Listen and complete the sentences. Where are these things? 🎧 *

1 crown

The Good Witch is wearing it on her head.

2 book

It's in the _____.

3 bottle

It's in the Wizard of Oz's _____.

4 jacket

The _____ is wearing it.

5 glasses

The _____ is wearing them.

6 ring

The _____ is wearing it.

* To complete this activity, listen to track 3 of the audio download available at www.ladybird.com/ladybirdreaders

11 Look at the pictures and read the questions. Who said this? Write the names on the lines.

Dorothy    scarecrow    tin man

Horrible Witch    lion

1 "I want to go back to Kansas. How do I get there?"

_____Dorothy_____

2 "I want to ask the wizard for some brains, so that I can think."

....

3 "I want to ask the wizard for a heart, so that I can love someone."

....

4 "I'm afraid of everyone and everything. I want the Wizard of Oz to make me brave."

....

5 "You horrible girl, your water is killing me!"

....

12 Look and read. These pictures are all the same. How are they the same? Choose the correct sentences and write them on the lines.

> They all want something.   They are all animals.
> They are all frightened.   They are all places to live.

1

They all want something.

2

_____

3

_____

4

_____

13 Look and read. Match the two parts of the sentences.

"If you go and kill the last Horrible Witch in Oz, — I will help you."

"If I have the magic shoes, — I will be the most horrible witch in Oz."

"If you don't give me your magic shoes, — I will kill your little dog."

"If you don't let us go, — I will throw this water over you."

"If you ask the shoes, — they will take you home."

14 Look and read. Write T (true) or F (false).

1 Everybody is happy. ......T.....

2 The wizard is holding Toto. ....

3 The Horrible Witch is in the picture. ....

4 The Good Witch is flying. ....

5 The lion, the tin man, and the scarecrow are saying goodbye. ....

6 Dorothy is going home. ....

15

15 Sing the song.

The storm carried Dorothy's house away,
far away to the country of Oz.
To go back home with Toto, her dog,
she had to see the Wizard of Oz.
She met the scarecrow who wanted a brain.
He had to see the Wizard of Oz.
They then met the tin man who wanted a heart.
He had to see the Wizard of Oz.
They then met a lion who wanted to be brave.
He had to see the Wizard of Oz.
In the Emerald City, they met a little man.
He took them to see the Wizard of Oz.

Everyone was frightened, but Dorothy spoke.
"What do you want?" said the Wizard of Oz.
They told him, and first they had to go and
kill the Horrible Witch—the last in Oz.
The witch wanted Dorothy's magic shoes
to make her the most horrible witch in Oz.
Dorothy threw water and killed the witch,
and they went back to see the Wizard of Oz.
"Now I can think!", "Now I can love!", "And now I am brave!"
said Dorothy's friends.
"How can I get home?" Dorothy asked.
She asked the shoes to take her and our story ends.

* To complete this activity, listen to track 4 of the audio download available at www.ladybird.com/ladybirdreaders